Playing Dead is Fun!

Jeremy Robertson

Copyright © 2021 by Jeremy Robertson

All Rights Reserved.

Contents

Chapter 1 : Living Well in Hell 1

Chapter 2 : A Little Halloween Humor 8

Chapter 3 : Partying with Poltergeists 15

Chapter 4 : Day for Slaying Dead Things 21

Chapter 5 : Miracle for Moon Goonies 28

Chapter 6 : Home for Halloween 33

Chapter 7 : No Way Out of Wishful Woods.. 39

Chapter 8 : Secrets of Jack's Spooky Soul Shack 44

Chapter 9 : Silly Zombies, You're Not Our Enemies! 51

ABOUT THE AUTHOR 57

Playing Dead is Fun!

Chapter 1 :
Living Well in Hell

I knew nothing good was going to happen to me on my next birthday party. In fact, I felt like canceling it. I didn't know what was going to happen. I just knew in my heart; I didn't feel like celebrating *any* parties. So many terrible things were going to happen to my family and friends. If I don't protect myself next Halloween, I may not survive it.

I was born on Halloween. Ever since my birth, I isolated myself from the world. Kept hearing secrets of the end of the world when I turn thirteen in a couple of weeks this year. I couldn't block out the voices in my head. Telling everybody would become reborn as an undead living corpse and walking the earth like zombies.

Jeremy Robertson

When I told my parents I wanted nothing to do with my birthday this year, they ignored me. They kept telling me how special I was. Even though they didn't understand how deeply sad I was over the years of my adolescences. They didn't help me. Figured it was stages I'm going through. I'd work out my problems.

Shows how much my folks cared about me. I wanted to play a joke with Mom and Dad and eleven-year-old kid sister, Tasha. They decorated the house for Halloween and my party they didn't seem to get my cancellation request. I wore make-up from head to toe to look like a dead zombie. And wrapped fake blooded sausages around my belly. To make it look like my guts got slashed open. And staggered into the living room as they were blowing up orange and black balloons.

Of course they didn't recognize me. Tasha screamed and Mom wrap her hug to protect her. Dad scrambled out of my way to get his shotgun he kept locked in a dresser drawer in the living room. When I realized he was going to shoot me, I held up my bloody hands in surrender. "Guys! Everybody! It's me, Teddy!" I explained, with a squeak in my voice. They didn't believe me right away. Dad continued to load his gun, and Mom gave me a funny look. Trying to realize it's me. After studying me for a moment, she nodded and told Dad to stand down.

"How can you be sure, Tabitha?" Dad asked. He walked toward me quickly and held the shotgun close to my dirty chest.

Mom walked closer to me, and she pointed at my face. "Because Todd. I noticed he's got two different colored eyes: blue on the left eye. Green eye on the right. See?" Centering me in the living room to see my different colored eyes, they gasped noticing it. Dad put away his protective gear.

"Why should we put up with your ridiculous behavior, Teddy?" Dad complained, locking the cabinet where he stored his household protective weapons. "You're going to end up dead, for real. Then what's next?" Dad yelled.

I felt angry. They weren't understanding me. "That's the point, Mom and Dad and Tasha! Once I become thirteen, I'll become undead. There's no stopping it. My blood cells in my body will become weak. And I will die at midnight on Halloween. And turn into a walking corpse! Believe me, please!" I demanded.

"Want us to send you to military school? Is that it? Your inappropriate behavior is inexcusable. No more talk about death! Your last birthday to be a kid is special and important to you. So, we're celebrating it, with or without you here!" Mom explained, harshly.

This wasn't fair! I screamed, silently. I let out an annoying groan. I unlatched the bloody sausages around my belly. And tossed in the trash. Then, ignoring my family, I walked out of the house. The night air was foggy and cold. We had scary carved faces of lighted jack-o'-lanterns lined up and down the steps of the pouch. I didn't wear a jacket or care if I'm still dressed like a freak. I stepped onto the porch and sat down at the wooden swing next to the front door.

The chilly wind blew fall leaves around in a circle on the front lawn. The front door opened, and my sister Tasha stepped out. She handed me a flashlight and a hot cup of chocolate. I thanked her but didn't feel like being around my family right now. I blew on the hot chocolate with white mini marshmallows in them and felt warm all over. Not at all like empty and eerie, like what's supposed to happen to me.

Tasha was shy like me. But she only cared about her family and friends the most. Like me, too. I didn't feel like facing my folks. Fearing they might ground me for giving everybody a good scare. Tasha looked at me and smiled wryly. "You're going to be okay; you know?" She admitted. I didn't believe her, but gave her a weak nod. Then took another sip of my hot chocolate. The marshmallows almost melted away before I could eat them.

"I know you all want what's best," I began, before taking another long sip of chocolate. "But Halloween is the one night, I will not be a twelve-year-old boy anymore," I said. "You can't stop what's going to happen. I don't want to scare everybody. But you've just got to believe something bad will happen to me on Halloween. It's the day I was born cursed with this power I'm not meant to have. If ya'll really love me, you'd stay away from me." I said, threatening her.

Tasha looked at me seriously for a moment. Not a crack of a smile on her face. I thought maybe I'd got the message to her head; I wasn't kidding around. Finally, Tasha let out a snorting laugh so hard, she toppled over the front porch. Holding her sides, she continued laughing and pointing at me. I felt my face grow red with embarrassment.

"You're looney tunes, bro," Tasha said, getting to a sitting position. "But I love ya and will do whatever you wish," she said. Tasha got to her feet and planted a kiss on my scabby forehead. And gave me a playful shove on the left shoulder. Then Tasha went back inside. I stayed on the swing, starry at the cloudy night sky.

A chill went through my body as I saw two kids appeared before our front porch, expressionless. They almost looked normal looking, except if it weren't for their very pale, dry skin and old-fashioned clothes they wore. They were a boy with curly red hair and freckles. And a blue-dyed haired girl, about my age. I didn't notice them at first. I thought they might my classmates. But they almost tempted me to hurry back in the safety on my house. Arms outstretched, they slowly staggered onto my front porch.

I hurried to go back inside, tossing the hot chocolate mug and flashlight at the two children. I swung open the door, turned to look back, and they both disappeared into thin air!

Chapter 2 :
A Little Halloween Humor

"Wake up, Sleepy Head!"

Parting open the draped curtains of my untidy bedroom window, Mom sang. The bright morning sunlight almost blinded me. She pulled the covers back off me. And shook me like a rag doll. "You've got a big day at school! You don't want to be late!" Mom continued sounding cheerful. She walked over to the closet and put an extra pair of brown kakis pants and clean light gray collared t-shirt out on my bed, beside my feet. She reached down to the closet on the floor and handed me a nice pair of brown leathered boots.

"Don't make me go!" I whined. I pulled the covers back over my head. Mom insisted I get dressed for school. She started

Playing Dead is Fun!

shaking and tickling me playfully. But when she tried to reveal the covers from my head. I scared the wits out of her. Because I wore an ugly, old werewolf Halloween mask. I burst out laughing as Mom collapse to the floor. "Please! Tell the principal I'm sick and can't attend my Halloween birthday party! I'll spread the disease I've caught to everybody else!" I complained.

Dad and Tasha entered my room. Tasha held a handheld camera in her hands and took my picture. Out popped the snap shot. Looking at the undeveloped photo, they waited to see what it looked like. "I hope I broke your *stupid* camera!" I snapped. I pulled the covers back over my head, desperate to get left alone.

But when I felt Tasha jumped on my bed and started tickling my sides, I knew the torture wasn't over. I got fed up with her fighting. Even though I knew she was playful. I sat up in bed and grew my poisonous vampire fangs, and took a bloody bite out of my sister's neck! Blood squirted on everybody. Tasha cried and fainted at the site her blood from my bite. My fangs slide back into my gums and disappeared. Mom and Dad helped Tasha put a band aide from a first aide kit next to my dresser on her neck. I grabbed her camera around her neck. And *flashed* her picture in front of her face. She blinked and tried reaching for the undeveloped snapshot. Already wounded and dizzy, Tasha wasn't giving up fighting me.

Mom and Dad grabbed us apart to separate our struggle. Dad grabbed the camera from me. And Mom took both snapshot photos of what we've token so far and put them on my dresser. "Now Ted. You're going to have fun today. I've got it all arranged with your homeroom teacher. You can spend the entire day until school's out to have your Halloween party. I set decorations in the school gym. You can play games; eat all the sweets you want. And hang out with your friends. I know how much stress you have felt because you think something bad will happen on your birthday. You're scared because you don't want to stop being a kid." Mom said, wholeheartedly.

I finally sat up and tried to get my family's attention. "You *don't* understand me! I *never* was a lucky kid, either! Why you think I've stuck out at night? Done nothing nice to my friends and family? I've lost interest in my hobbies. I just want to disappear off the face of the earth!" I explained, sprawling my face over my pillow with an annoying groan.

Looking at me disappointingly, Mom and Dad stood in front of me with their arms cross. "Either that, or get grounded for two weeks. Do chores around the house and no fun of any kind!" Dad explained, cruelty. I gulped, and I knew he was serious because they weren't smiling or taking their eyes off me. I looked at Mom and Dad, then I saw Tasha in the back beside them. She was making funny faces at me and pointing fingers at our parents. I couldn't help but burst out laughing.

Mom and Dad seemed confused as they whirled around and faced Tasha. She folded her eyes quickly and began whistling nervously. "This goes for you too, Tasha," Mom scolded her. Even though Mom didn't know what she did. Tasha nodded and gulped, but understood. "You're invited as well. But if the two of your antics continue, *nobody* will have fun around, *anymore*!" Mom explained, her voice got loud and angry.

Jeremy Robertson

A few moments later, I got pre-ready for my Halloween school party. Dad drove my sister Tasha and I in our big, green suburban vehicle at our local high school. He pulled into the parking lot, where kids were in their Halloween costumes awaiting my arrival. I was nervous about it. I knew I'm supposed to a fun, frightening time. But something bad was going to happen. And I didn't know how to stop it.

A couple of my good high school buddies Marco Drag (dressed in a sweet Dracula costume complete with pale make-up. He wore very sharp fangs and wore a long, silky black cape and all.) Jason Bug (dressed as Frankenstein's monster. He wore a black tuxedo with green make-up and bolts on the side of his forehead.) They walked up to the car and started spraying Silly String with pink and green colors at us! Dad honked his horn, excited to see my friends having fun already. He waved at them. All my classmates applauded as they walked closer to our car.

Dad walked out of the driver's side. He opened the front passenger's side and escorted me out. I opened the door for Tasha. My sister looked great in her costume. She dressed as the princess

Playing Dead is Fun!

in the *Super Mario Bros.* Nintendo video games. Complete with a yellow tiara and pink slippers, silky dress, and all.

Dad gave my friends and schoolmates high fives. Even though I knew he's sometimes *overly* friendly with them, it just embarrasses me. I looked away and tried not to feel humiliated. Suddenly, Dad ruffled my neatly combed hair and gave me a sharp hug too tight. I struggled to breathe. Tasha took my picture with her camera and it made me cry out and see spots. That's why Tasha's at my party so she can take all the stupid photos of me at my birthday party doing *stupid* stuff.

"My birthday boy's here! Show him how to have fun, really!" Dad explained happily to my friends and classmates. They mostly laughed and jumped up and down for joy, mostly to annoy me in front of my Dad and sister. I wanted it to be over before it begun!

I huddled behind Dad and climb back in the passenger's seat. Tasha quickly noticed me. And *slapped* the front door in my face! I cringed and almost got my hands jammed! Everybody thought that was a riot and laughed more.

Marco and Jason started grabbing hold of me and dragged me into the school. "Pick you up after the party, Teddy and Tasha!" Dad called after me, waving. He walked back into the car and drove off. Where I knew I would not have fun at all!

Chapter 3 :
Partying with Poltergeists

No matter how many times I begged my friends I didn't want to play any games with them, they ignored me. "It's my birthday! I'll cry if I want too!" I complained. Not my best original combat, but they finally obeyed me. I took a seat in the middle of the bleachers or the decorated gym, as my two best friends Marco and Jason joined me.

"What is wrong, buddy?" Marco asked. I didn't know want to talk about it. So I looked away from my friends. Marco and Jason put a comforting hand around my shoulder. "We're here to have fun! Relax! It's your birthday! Anything bad happens to you, we'll protect you." Marco promised.

Suddenly, the black colored lightning flickered and dimmed. The deejay pointed a spotlight at my face. I held out at my hand in defense and turned away. The jock spoke into the microphone as it screeched to life. "Alright, ladies and monsters! Let's get the birthday boy something to scream about!" He cranked up loud pop music. Then, he pointed the yellow spotlight to his lady friend Rebecca Realtro at the snack bar.

Turning red from embarrassment, they knew I had a secret crush on Rebecca since third grade. Rebecca dressed in a white ghostly, glowing white gown, like a wedding dress. And wore a silver cross necklace and looked flattered. She batted her eyes. As she accepted two plastic cups of fruit punch to her. Marco and Jason looked innocently at each other. Then, gripping hold of me around the arms, they led me off the blenchers. And onto the foggy dance floor, next to the snack bar.

"No! You can't do this to me!" I screamed. But ignoring my cries of defeat, they forced me to join Rebecca and her group of girlfriends. "Huh, sup?" My voice squeaked. And everybody laughed. Including Rebecca. Which made me feel even more embarrassed. Rebecca handed me the red fruit punch cup. I looked at and gasped. It looked like thick, blood! I sat it aside on the table next to us, and so did my lady friend. I took her by the hand and soft rock music played. We walked to the middle of the dance floor. Where colorful disco lights flashed above our heads.

"You don't want to be with me, really? Do you?" I asked. She glared at me. And *pushed* me away from me. Then Rebecca *slapped* me across the side of the face! It sting and it got incredibly quiet. The jock music stopped playing. And everybody surrounded us. Waiting for a response.

I suddenly got very tense. "You're *my* boyfriend!" She explained, madly. "You may be dead inside, but I loved you from the moment I noticed your dead flaky skin. Did I think anything different from you because you *were* different?" Rebecca asked. I remained silent again. Unable to hide my emotions. Everybody seemed to stare at us. All eyes turned to me. The deejay pointed the spotlight on my face.

I cringed and flinched away from the bright light. "You're not afraid of me?" I said, sadly. Rebecca took my decaying, scabby green hands and planted a sweet kiss on each hand. I small tear slowly escaped my left eye. "I live my life in sin. It could destroy your soul, too," I said.

Letting out a nervous laughter, Rebecca dried my tears. "Let me share you my story," She asked. We all took a long, disturbed pause. "I'm a Soul Snatcher. I can give life a second chance. When somebody's suffering, I can give them peace after snatching their souls from this!" She grabbed a gold pocket mirror out of her pink purse with a gold chain she wore around her shoulder. "It's a Miracle Mirror!" she explained. Hoping up the glowing golden mirror, everybody forced to look away before opening it, including me.

"Put that away!" one of her best girlfriend's snapped. A silver, glowing light almost escaped from the inside of Rebecca's Miracle Mirror as it bounced off the ceiling and hit the spinning disco ball. Rebecca and I quickly shut the lid of her magic glass.

Playing Dead is Fun!

"This all must be a grim joke," I said, glumly. "When do we suddenly live in a world where only monsters exist in it?" I asked. Marco and Jason bumped chests and started playing, fighting with each other, not giving a care. But I felt deadly serious. Using my sudden super strength I didn't realize I had, I split my friends apart to stop the violence. "Guys! We all must get along! Or none of us will know the truth about the Monster Kingdom." I said, loudly. My big voice echoed across the suddenly quiet basketball gym.

Taking a sweet, caramel coated candy apple off a platter on the party table, Marco took a big bite and chewed and smacked nosily. "Right, kid. You expect we're all some part of *Monster Kingdom*? Reality is just a figment of our imagination because it's so boring to you. What if we think *you're* boring if we don't want to be your friends anymore?" Marco asked, snacking on the candy apple.

I looked at Marco and *slapped* the candy apple away from him. It rolled up the party table and looked at me crazily. Like he and all my friends wanted to get into a fight. My sister Tasha suddenly thought this is humorous. She flashed her camera at us as Marco tried strangling me. Trying not to get beat up by my friends, I suddenly felt starving. I took a *big* bite out of Marco's arm that was choking me to death. He staggered back, looking at his bloody wound.

Tasha took another picture of Marco's wound and slapped a high five with Rebecca. "Guys! Guys! Everybody! Get along or I'll kick everybody out!" We turned to look as Principal Staggers, dressed as a grown-up Peter Pan costume (aka *Hook*), entered the basketball gym. We all moaned and turned to our disappointment because Mr. Staggers was the only adult friend in the building. "Hey ya'll, I'm cool! Watch this!" He showed taking out a pouch of fairy dust from his green pants pocket, he sprinkled fairy dust over himself. And started flying in the air and under the disco ball. He pointed to the deejay, and he played loud pop music again. "Let's get this party started!" He said excitedly. And started doing a disco dance under the glowing ball.

We just knew it were to get much worse. And there's nothing we could do about it.

Playing Dead is Fun!

Chapter 4 :
Day for Slaying Dead Things

I wanted the party to end before it even began. Rebecca couldn't stop clinging onto me during the entire dance. I begged my friends silently to get me out of this alive. Even though it seemed too late for that. Marco and Jason were playing a game of "Hot Potato" with a red rubber dodge ball. At the other end of the gym with the rest of my classmates. Marco tossed the dodge ball high in the air to hard and fast and *smacked* Jason in the gut. Nearly knocking the wind out of his breath. Jason got his breath, and they both broke into a riot and bumped chests together. Everybody else applauded and cheered as well.

Gripping hold of the dodge ball, Jason tossed it back as their friend Stacy Maggot dressed in green alien makeup and costume. She lost her grip on the ball, and it rolled away from the group.

And the dodge ball rolled its way toward Rebecca and me. Marco and Jason encouraged the two of us to play a quick game. Rebecca rolled her eyes and the rowdy kids. She kicked the ball back toward them. Cringing in pain because it stumped her toe. "We're busy here!" She yelled, sticking her tongue out at them.

As much as I wanted to join my friends, Rebecca quickly wrapped her arms around me. Her eyes didn't stop staring at me. "I'm sorry. I can't do this," I said. Trying to break up our tense relationship. "I need some air." I explained walking away from my girlfriend.

I walked out the gym where I met Principal Staggers talking with the friendly janitor Mr. Scabs. He mopped up the white linoleum floor. But he stopped, and they turned to look at me. "Birthday dude! Did you score?" Principal Staggers. Mr. Scabs laughed and rested on the mop and starred at me, dreamily.

I didn't feel like talking about it. "I just want to go home. Can you give me a ride, Principal Staggers?" I asked, hoarsely. Without hesitation, Mr. Staggers nodded and agreed. He turned to look at Mr. Crossbones. "It's almost midnight. I'll be in trouble if I don't make it on time." I said.

"Can you lock up early? Tell the kids the party's over," Principal Staggers explained. Nodding, Mr. Crossbones put the wet, soapy mop back into the yellow bucket. Mr. Crossbones walked into the gym and let out a high-pitched scream! Mr. Staggers and I turned to enter the gym to see what went wrong.

"What?!" Mr. Staggers asked. Suddenly, my sister Tasha walked up close to us with a worried expression. We gasped and looked shock at her shredded princess dress. She held up her camera and showed them her recent snap shot photo. Before we could see what, the commotion was going on, Tasha pushed us out of the way. And back out into the school hallway.

"They all went *crazy*!" Tasha cried, almost tripping over her pink dress. "I think it was the disco ball. With the deejay playing loud creepy, elevator music. It turned them mad. Destroying the decorations. Fighting with each other. Not getting along. I'm the only not affected by the disco ball. I took proof before I escaped,"

Tasha said. She held up the black-and-white photo and slowly watched it develop.

Finally, the photo revealed a green monster hand holding an orange crepe paper with the words in black marker: BOO! Silence. Then, a blast of wind from the double basketball gym doors opened, blowing the snapshot out of Tasha's reach. We turned and watched as Rebecca ran hurriedly out first, screaming bloody murder. Her dress all wrinkled and dirty. Turning to face me, she quickly wrapped her arms around me.

"We have to go! Get out of here! NOW!" Rebecca demanded, shrilly. I turned to look nervously into the gym. But Rebecca insisted it's not safe. "We can't help them. Halloween is alive," she said. It made little sense of what my girlfriend talked about. I just knew whatever happened was real. And it terrified the living daylights out of Rebecca.

Taking the end of the mop, Mr. Crossbones stuck it through the double doors. Hoping to keep the monsters trapped. But it wouldn't be for long. Because they tried breaking it down with their super strength. They almost pushed it open so hard and fast, they almost cracked the wooden mop broom.

"What happened?" I asked, terrified of the truth. We all raced down the hall trying to get out of the school. The lights flickered but didn't go all the way out. Rebecca took out her Miracle Mirror from her small pink purse. Snapping it open, she tried not to look at her own reflection in the light as it nearly pulled her own soul into magic charm. She snapped it and put it back in her purse. But lost her grip, and it went sailing across the slippery floor.

Scrambling to get, they all failed to grab for Rebecca's Miracle Mirror as it went under the crack door of the teacher's lounge. Principal Staggers told everybody to remain calm. He grabbed out his keys from his pocket and unlocked the door. It squeaked open and there they saw the Miracle Mirror a few inches in front of them.

Mr. Staggers bent down, grabbed the magic mirror, and handed it to Rebecca. "Tell us what you know," Mr. Staggers said. Rebecca turned red. She looked away from us and tried not to hide her emotions. "It's okay, child. You can be straight with us." He said.

Rebecca dried her tears away. "I don't know. I just putting make-up on, while looking through my Miracle Mirror. The next thing I knew, the light reflected off it. And made everyone a little, not their selves. We have to get Ted home before Halloween curses him to," she said, looking at me seriously. "Or you'll become a permanent midnight monster as well." Rebecca said, sadly. I didn't know what to think. Except everybody has gone totally mad. And it's all my fault.

"We won't make it to my house on time," I said. "We just have half-hour left on the clock. The only way to break the spell would be to wait till daylight in a safe place. Like the church or something. It's down the block. Now, I'm unholy, but maybe the Almighty Father can accept all His children until I can be my normal, soul again," I said, thoughtfully.

They looked at me expressionless. "Our Father might not want sinful creatures of the night into his house of worship," Mr.

Playing Dead is Fun!

Staggers said. "It's a plan worth trying. Let's go," They walked out the school building, not long before the hungry, violent Halloween monsters broke the mop stick holding the basketball gym door, storming after them.

Jeremy Robertson

Chapter 5 :
Miracle for Moon Goonies

A reflection of the bright, orange glowing full moon appeared in a watery mud puddle in the middle of the foggy street. I stepped in the puddle as the water rippled and made them vanish into the shadows of the night. I looked over my shoulder and discovered the slow-moving monsters from the high school parking lot were still coming after us.

I started panting and out of breath. "There's got to be a faster way," I said, breathlessly. Mr. Staggers pointed to the big, yellow school bus in the school parking lot. He pointed at it and we all ran toward it. But as Mr. Staggers tried opening the sliding doors, it wouldn't budge. Finally, after tugging hard, it swung open. And out shot a very pale hand with sharp, gnarly fingers *punch* Mr.

Playing Dead is Fun!

Staggers in the face. Making the principal and us stumble backwards onto the cold, damp ground.

A pair of glowing red eyes starred back at us. "You're making a big mistake," a deep, raspy voice said. Trying to give us a good scare. And it worked, because as I looked into the shadowy darkness of the school bus, the voice belonged to the priest, Father Moonshine! He stepped onto the first step of the bus. His eyes haunted me the most because they were pools of solid black pupils. The glowing reflection of the Miracle Moon reflected in them when he turned to look at it. Then he quickly turned to look right at me! And his eyes turned black and evil.

"What's happening?" I squeaked. We tried to check on Mr. Staggers. But he wasn't conscious. We helped the principal to a sitting position as if we were all getting soaked from the rain.

"Do you really want to know?" Father Moonshine asked, his voice even robust and haunting us as ever. He took another step off the bus. "You've awakened the ritual of Moon Goonie Gods thanks to your unappreciative Halloween birthday party. You have no choice to unleash your power. Your Halloween ghost will be free to make this holiday feel even more alive than ever. It's time to join me with the Moon Goonie Gods on the let the celebration of the afterlife journey begin!" The priest proclaimed, dramatically. He tossed his long arms in the air as he a bolt of lightning struck the sky. Followed by a drum roll of deep thunder, making us all grovel before him.

The Moon Goonies were closing in on us. I could feel their need for wanting to feed and destroy our very souls. I wasted no more valuable time. "Okay! Let's go, Father!" I screamed, scrambling past him. Making our way into the school bus. Just as Father Moonshine shut the bus doors, the Moon Goonies tried breaking and smashing into the bus. They mashed and pounded on the windows. But Father Moonshine and I tried to block them out by locking the doors and staying away from the windows.

We mostly tried keeping in the shadows. While Moon Goonies tried rocking and toppling us over. The sound of the back door smashed open. We turned and screamed behind us. We watched as Moon Goonie, looking like a big, evil turned Donkey

Playing Dead is Fun!

Kong character from the Nintendo video games, entered from the back door. He noticed Rebecca and I clenching onto to each other for dear life.

Father Moonshine tried to step in front of us. When the big ape let out a roar of thunder. Eyes flashed red. And *snapped* Father Moonshine's neck, breaking it like a toothpick. My friends and girlfriend, let out a bloodcurdling scream. Marco and Jason held on to each other for dear life. Jason gasped with fright and fainted. There wasn't much I could do to help us escape as evil Monkey Man *snatched* my girlfriend out of my arms. And went out the emergency exit, pounding his chest and laughing like an outsized hairy monkey man. I watched helplessly as monkey Man raced deep into end of town, where the spooky woods began. He raced up the trees, carrying my screaming girlfriend over his shoulders. While there isn't a thing, I could do about it.

The Moon Goonies started grabbing hold of my friends. And dragging or carrying them out of the school bus. They weren't interested in me. Or Father Moonshine, he's finished already. Marco tried to fight against the evil Halloween monsters, wearing a Monster Mask. The creature's haunting, narrow eyes tried hypnotizing Marco. He looked at me for help. But the other Moon Goonies held all of us hostages.

Breaking free of their grasp, Marco tried removing the villain's Monster Mask. Searching for a line around the back of its neck, it remained on his face, like it's his skin. Laughing ironically, Monster Mask's eyes flashed yellow. So did Marco's eyes, and he went into a goofy, dreamy state. Monster Mask caught Marco around his waist, and the rest of the Moon Goonies continued taking my friends to the Wishful Woods. There, *nobody's* safe. Where Monkey Man will have a much bigger miracle for the Moon Goonies.

I wouldn't even be a part of it.

Chapter 6 :
Home for Halloween

It seemed after the night of my Halloween party; it didn't seem like it happened. Dad came by the school later that night and took me home. I didn't know how to explain to my dad what all's going on here. Especially with me. Because it seemed like I wanted this weird fantasy of becoming unreal not to end anymore. Now I'm thirteen. Officially, a preteen with a wild nature of a problem.

Dad kept glancing at me every time he slowed to a stoplight. "What's wrong, kid? Really?" Dad asked, turning his blinker on at the stoplight. "You can't get away with silence forever. If you're hiding some dark, terrible secret. I'm going to find out. I don't want to punish you for something you're innocent of. Mom didn't pick up Tasha. She's worried sick about us. So please, kid.

Come clean. And tell me what's bothering you," Dad said. He turned right at the stoplight when it turned green.

"What do you want me to say?" I asked, my throat felt parched and dry. "All I wanted was a Halloween birthday party celebration, not to feel forgotten. That's what I got. Because something happened to my sister and friends. You think it's my fault for causing them to get in this whole big accident I don't have an explanation for? I'm responsible for them. But I know it will not make it right without my proof of the Halloween curse. You *don't* get me. *I* don't understand myself." I said, quietly. In fact, I didn't feel like talking the rest of the drive home.

Dad pouted but kept his eyes on the road and turned on the radio to Christian music. It keeps him feeling peaceful under stress. I knew my living dead corpse wouldn't survive long enough until the next craving. I knew I didn't want to think about it. Because as I concentrated on Dad's driving, I suddenly started feeling starving. I could hear his heart beating. Dad looked at me and noticed my face started sweating and looked paler than ever. "Are you feeling yourself?" Dad asked. He took his right hand

and put on my forehead. When suddenly, I *snapped*—and grabbed Dad's hand. And took a *big* bite out of his hand!

Blood splattered all over the dashboard and our clothes. Dad swerved at the steering wheel and we *crashed* into a red fire hydrant at the nearby sidewalk! Water erupted and spewed everywhere. I knew I made a terrible mistake by taking a bite out of Dad's hand. But if I didn't control the hunger soon, it would consume my unwanted soul!

Dad tried to fight back. I stopped what I did and tried to apologize. But the horrified deed got done. Dad's hand got bloody wounded by mistake. "WHY?" Dad bellowed at the top of his lungs, sobbing. And trying to stop the pain. "YOU ARE NOT MY SON!" Dad screamed more. And fumbled out the passenger door and stumbled onto the wet street pavement.

"Dad, I can explain," I let out a burb. "I had to do it. Because you could become what I am. An undead demon who craves human flesh. To become undead, go through the Moon Goonie ritual. You can get stronger if you feed on Tasha's brain. She doesn't need it. Mostly because she doesn't have one. Now, we have little time to rescue her and my friends from Donkey Kong and the Moon Goonies. The Monkey Man took Tasha and the other kids to Wishful Woods. Doing who knows what? To join the fun, we must get there before Halloween curses me to be undead forever. We have till sunrise to save the day," I said with a bloody stained grin on my face.

Dad didn't pay any attention. He sauntered slowly over my the sprouting dehydrant and washed the blood from his wound. "Dad, listen! To get your hand back, feed on my dumb sister's brains! Either way, you'll die from your critical condition. I didn't *want* to do it. But I would only suffer more if we all don't sacrifice the Moonie Goonies." I said. Dad slowly tried walking away from me as I advanced closer. "Dad, don't make this hard," I complained.

Dad grabbed a walking stick off the street and started swinging at my face. "NO! I am NOT an evil walking dead! I will NEVER be like YOU!" Dad continued swinging the big, curvy walking stick at my face. I dodged quickly, even though I am undead. I grabbed the stick out of Dad's reach and *snapped* it in half. And tossed it aside. Dad held onto his wounded hand, crying as I slowly wrapped Dad in a hug. He might think I would eat the rest of him.

"I'm already full for the night," I said. Dad looked at me uncertainly. "You, however, have until sunrise to feed on human flesh. Once Mom and Tasha get turned next, we can defeat the Moon Goonies from permanently turning the rest of the townspeople into zombie dust. Break their spell, and we'll be human!" I explained, happily. Even though I knew it wouldn't get Dad easy to join the ranks of the undead, to save a few innocent lives, he would get a change of heart by the end of the night.

"We'll be alright, once we're home for Halloween," I said, taking Dad by his other healthy hand. I looked at Dad's wounded other hand. It didn't look pretty. Dad wobbled around my arms as we walked toward the shadowy entrance to Wishful Woods. I could hear screams and cries of defeat as we got closer. I glanced at the entrance where a pair of sinister, spooky, glowing yellow eyes stared back at us in greeting. I heard it giggling and taunting us to come closer.

Dad looked at me suspiciously. He suddenly had a change of courage and walked up to the floating pair of eyes. "You don't know us. What we can do. We wish to enter peacefully. Or enter a world of ugly," Dad said, forcefully. I didn't know what to think. Dad's sudden change of bravery made me want to root for him.

Suddenly, the yellow pair of eyes blinked twice. And floated in the air and vanished. A clearing parted away for us. Unexpectedly, something drifted in front of our faces! We screamed and tried batting it away from us. It started giggling strangely at the two of us. I realized what it appeared to be: A spirit guide! We followed the friendly ball of light in the shadows of the unknown. Where we would *not* feel welcomed in Wishful Woods.

Chapter 7 :
No Way Out of Wishful Woods

Once Dad and I entered Wishful Woods, the sound of thorn bushes sealed the entrance. Blocking our only chance of getting out. We gasped with startlement, as we heard sinister laughter in the darkness of the trees. The glowing, evil pair of eyes in the shadows starred back at us.

Dad and I concentrated on following the spirit guide, but it too disappeared. We looked for a path to walk on. But all we could see is our shadows from the glow of the full moon shinning down from the top of the trees. Suddenly, the branches blew apart slowly. Then, the moonlight shone a path to lead into the heart of the woods. Dad wrapped an arm around my shoulder. And we wobbled our way into the darkness.

"Try not to think about pain, Dad," I explained. He nodded and put his wounded right hand against his chest. To keep the throbbing, searing heartache from worsening. "Don't stare into the Evil Eyes, either. They'll lure you into their death trap." I said.

Dad wobbled on his legs and felt weak with wry. "We have to rest. I don't want to go any further, Ted," Dad said, breathlessly. Suddenly, storm clouds cover the bright full moon. We got plunged into shadows again. I could tell the Evil Eyes staring at us in their lair, we're enjoying giving us a good scare.

I could hear a wild animal somewhere in the core of Wishful Woods howling. Many kinds of unknown dangers were a threat. Dad and looked around for the spirit guide to return. But when we a young girl scream bloody murder, it almost seemed like it belonged to Tasha! With no more reaction, Dad and I sprinted full speed ahead into Wishful Woods.

When Dad and I reached the end of the path of the clearing, the full moonlight shone a patch of sunniness on a swamp hermit, a small wooden shack. We reached the hut, when suddenly the angry spirit guide flew out of the peephole. It appeared as a shadowy death skull. And warned us to stay away in a crispy sounding voice. Then vanished into our faces as it turned to ash.

Suddenly, Monkey Man and Tasha walked out the shack, like they were happily dating each other. When they stopped to notice us, they looked spooked. Tasha dropped the yellow flower Monkey Man gave him. The big ape narrowed his eyes at them and pumped his hairy knuckles at his fists.

"It's okay, Mr. Monkey Man," Tashs flushed with embarrassment. "They're family. They think we need saving or something," she laughed. Monkey Man narrowed his hairy eyebrows at them. He stood beside her like the dominate male protecting his female mate.

Tasha looked at me and then at Dad. She gasped when she noticed his wounded hand and we got covered in his blood. "What the dickens?!" she gasped. "Was there an accident?" Dad and I looked at Tasha with stink eyes. "I get it. So, what's going on? Why are all of us acting like a bunch of weirdos?" she asked.

I didn't know where to explain. Or why it's happening to us. I only knew it's something we're going to get used to. Tasha tapped her pink slipper on the dirt pavement, impatiently. "We've got time," she said, finally. Dad started looking a little undead like me. Because of my attack. He starred Tasha like a four-course meal. I heeled Dad to control his animal instincts.

I inhaled a deep breath and sighed to explain. "Okay. So the Halloween spirit is with us now. Everything you thought couldn't exist is becoming real. I infected Dad already with my undead venom. We got until sunrise to turn the rest of our family into zombies. Or we'll become dead dust in the afterlife, forever. We don't want to go there. Until we can our human selves, we must feed on a body part of each family member. The Moon Goonies don't know what's happened to them as well from my Halloween party. They think they're meant like that. We must get it right for everybody before sunset. Or my Halloween spirit could destroy humanity," I said.

"I don't want that to happen!" Tasha snapped. She turned to Monkey Man, who didn't take his stink eyes off me. "Love, I'm sorry. But I must go on a mission. It's a family emergency. Collect your buddies. We're going to have the best time of our lives at the Monster Kingdom!" Tasha bellowed, throwing her arms in the air, excitedly.

Before Tasha could join us, Monkey Man snatched Tasha around her waist. And hoisted her over his broad, hairy shoulders. And grabbed a tree vine and swung deeper in the woods, screaming the whole way.

"This is going to be harder than we thought," I told Dad. He agreed. As undead zombie hands started reaching out at us from the shadowy trees in Wishful Woods. We bolted away from the path and entered Monkey Man's empty shack, cowering in a corner. We cried in vain as we heard the horrible animal sounds from the Moon Goonies, desperate to get in. Not realizing just how to get out of this alive.

Chapter 8 :
Secrets of Jack's Spooky Soul Shack

"**F**ather, I'm so scared!" I said. We clung onto each other for dear life. No matter what we tried to do to feel safe, one of the strong, undead Moon Goonies *punched* a hole in the front wooden door. Shadows danced around us and as the slow-moving zombies charged after us!

Dad looked for a weapon. He spotted a red tool chest under the bench next to us. He quickly grabbed for it. Missed. Tried grabbing it again. Missed again. Slipped from his fingers. And before he could try again, a nearby Moon Goonie *swiped* the toolbox out of his reach. We groaned in defeat. The zombie looked pleased he is pestering with us.

Playing Dead is Fun!

The Moon Gonnie holding the red toolbox dumped out its contests. Instead of finding tools, something else *plopped* out of it onto the dirt ground. We couldn't tell what it appeared at first. But the zombies quickly grabbed for it. It looked like a necklace, a black pendant. An upside down cross carved on it.

The Moon Goonies surrounding us gasped in shock as the pendant glowed as the leader of the Moon Goonies wore it around its scrawny, scabby neck. A golden light washed over him, and the creature became human! Dad and I didn't know how to respond. But the other Moon Goonies seemed to grovel before him. He looked like a twenty-year-old rock star. He wore stylish clothes and a brown leather coat. Taking out his hand, the Moon Goonie held out his hand to help us to our feet.

We were reluctant at first. But the Monster Leader grabbed hold of our hands in an extraordinarily firm grip. And pulled us to our feet. "Who *are* you? Should we be afraid?" Dad asked. I wanted to know myself. But by the unfriendly smile on the Monster Leader's face, I could tell he isn't somebody we should trust.

"Hello, my friends! I'm Jack the Monster Leader! Here to save you all," he introduced himself, cheerfully. Still with an ornery grin on his face. "Welcome to my Soul Shack. A magical place where you can understand what it feels like to be an *actual* monster!" Jack explained. Suddenly, his necklace started stinging him.

"What's wrong?" I asked, trying to stay away from the other still, evil Moon Goonies beside Dad and me.

"It seems the Monster Kingdom is losing hope of protecting the sinister souls of the Moon Goonies from ever remembering what it's like to be human," Jack said. He realized the hungry zombies were starring at how tasty Jack the Monster Locker looked. Because he seemed so full of hearty protein. Dad and I tried to control the Moon Goonie's untamed behavior.

When a nearby zombie took a bite out of Dad's neck, I twirled around and *cracked* its neck. The other Moon Goonies trembled in our presence. As Jack grabbed of his black, shadowy pendant to restrain them.

Playing Dead is Fun!

"The only thing on a monster's mind, is food," Jack said. "But they can't hurt us in my Soul Shack. There's a magical barrier protecting those like us, who are innocent. We need to get them back to the Monster Kingdom. And bring them food source so it will satisfy their hunger for soul food." He said, angrily. Pressing hold of his pendant against an ugly, female Moon Goonie who tried biting Jack's leg.

"You said they *can't* hurt us here!" Dad snapped. As the mad zombie mob continued shoving us around, violently.

Jack looked like he sounded dumb. Then he clarified himself. "What I meant was: They can still *try* to harm us. But with we figure out how to tame them, they'll ignore us. Until we can find out what their source of soul food is." Jack said, looking around the crowded Soul Shack. Suddenly, Jack spotted a box of silver metal bracelets on a wooden worktable where the fighting, hostile Moon Goonies wrestled over them.

Dad, Jack, and I went over to the worktable. We each frantically grabbed a single metal bracelet from the box. "We do we do?" I asked, thoughtfully. Dad and I began tossing each other the bracelets away from the mob of Moon Goonies as they swarmed around us to get them. Dad and I weren't sure what the purpose of these magic bracelets was for.

"These are Behavior Bracelets," Jack said. Before a misunderstood zombie could swipe it out of Jack's reach, Jack quickly twirled around it. And *snapped* the charmed bracelet on the hungry Moon Goonie's right wrist. He began blinking green, rapidly. Then stopped and flashed red lights. The zombie's eyes turned red and behaved in a paralyzed state of mind. It blinked, and he suddenly appeared to have human characteristics on his face.

The goofy zombie almost stumbled and fell. But we caught the monster's balance. "Jack? Is it you? What's going on, buddy?" The Moon Goonie had a high-pitched voice. Like the sound of a squeaky dog chew toy. I couldn't help but snicker at how almost cute he sounded.

Playing Dead is Fun!

Suddenly, the other zombies turned and noticed the good zombie wearing the Behavior Bracelet and it controlled him from feeding on human flesh. "Everybody! Put on the enchanted bracelets! It helps control our hunger. I feel completely normal now!" The good Moon Goonie named Hunter said.

Some younger kid-looking Moon Goonies didn't know how to put on the Behavior Bracelets. So we helped them. Until every undead zombie wore one. They began acting more human. Hunter turned to Jack's attention. "Is there a cure for us, Jack? Please, tell us you know how to get us back to normal," Hunter asked.

The other Moon Goonies started talking at once. Getting excited about returning to a normal life. "Calm down, everybody. Relax!" Jack yelled. We all huddled close to him. Jack looked uneasy, and he said for everybody to take their distances. "Bad news. The world you've come from–Monster Kingdom–is no longer of existence. It seems you can blame this kid here, Teddy, for losing his imagination to believe in it. Because he's become like you all on his birthday. So there is no cure and no way back home. An order to move on, you'd have to obey the laws of reality here in the actual world. I'm sorry, but there is nothing I can do for you all now, anymore. Continue to wear the Behavior Bracelets and you'll learn it's your only way of survival. I'm off to my world to have fun. Teddy is your new Monster Leader," Jack stormed off before any of us could get him to explain the truth about the world of unwanted evil.

They all turned to look at me with a forceful vengeance, waiting for instructions. I gulped and Dad and I ran after Jack. We're so *not* prepared for what happened next.

Chapter 9 :
Silly Zombies, You're Not Our Enemies!

While Dad and I hurried out of the Soul Shack, a beam of yellow light flashed over us. Closing our eyes, we blinked twice. It took a moment to realize what happened. In the blink of an eye, we got surrounded by a bunch of decent looking zombies throwing a party. They had the clearing of Wishful Woods decorated with colorful balloons and streamers hanging down from the tree branches. The fun bunch of Moon Goonies even had noise makers. And they danced choreographically offbeat to the blaring music. When Hunter, the first Moon Goonie to wear the Behavior Bracelet, greeted us by the refreshment table. Loud pop music blared over by the deejay, next to the large, square wooden table. He waved at us, too.

Hunter and his three undead friends, who are a boy and two girls, gathered next to us. "The Land of the Unliving invited us to our celebration party!" Hunter explained. He had a noise maker in his hand and blew it. "As long as we are in a friendly behavior, they can't banish us to the Zombie Zone for eternity," Hunter said, smiling mischievously.

I didn't know what to say. I realized I didn't wear a Behavior Bracelet. I still got infected with decaying cells rotting my soul away. If I don't get one right away, I could do something evil. My stomach started growling and the four friendly Moon Goonies gasped and stepped away from me. I looked at them innocently. Dad also got infected with cursed blood because I bite his right hand. And he, too, could turn against the entire Monster Kingdom.

"Get Jack here!" snapped Hunter's good friend, Thomas Space. "Ted and Todd both aren't wearing Behavior Bracelets! They're turning into one of us, fast!" Thomas screamed like a whiny girl and ran off, deep into the dark unknown of Wishful Woods.

Playing Dead is Fun!

Looking after him Hunter, and the rest of us remained calm. "What a wimp," Hunter's black female friend, next to him on the left named, Tonya said. "Jack's recently retired. He's on vacation. Don't worry, dudes. We'll get you a bracelet." She walked over to the refreshment table. The red toolbox where they kept extra pairs of Behavior Bracelets, next to the fruit punch bowl, vibrated.

All the Moon Goonies bracelets they were buzzing and blinking red. Hunter, Tonya, and the other undead friend named Christina started doubling over in agony. Grabbing their stomach, they realized it's feeding time.

"Wait! Let me get Jack!" I shouted. Running out into the shadowy path leading into Wishful Woods, I got stopped. Before I knew it, I realized who came to save the day: Mom and my sister. Driving our family vehicle into the clearing path, the Moon Goonies discovered this as an opportunity for a snack. They quickly swarmed our car.

Before they could lock their doors, the monsters tried opening them. Breaking the windows. Scratching up the vehicle. Slashing their big, black tires until they became flat. Hunter, Tonya, and Christina grabbed hold of Dad and me. My heart pounded badly. I could tell Dad didn't know how to survive, either.

Suddenly, making wild animal sounds coming from the darkness of Wishful Woods, Monkey Man returned with Rebecca carrying her shoulders. They did a wild flip in the air as they leaped onto the nutrition table. But as they were both heavy and strong, the table creaked and broke in pieces. Maing the snacks and drinks fall to the ground. Monkey Man kindly helped Rebecca to her feet.

Monkey Man started swinging his huge, muscular arms and tossing the Moon Goonies out of the car's way. Mom and Tasha screamed, and they couldn't tell what they got into themselves. Rebecca got out her Miracle Mirror from her purse. While Dad and they held me hostage, Rebecca opened her Miracle Mirror. A flash of silver light shined from it. Then, a bright light reached its wispy hand toward Hunter, Christina, and Tonya. The ghostly claw went into their eyes. They blinked and slobbered all over their chin. Then slumped to the ground in defeat.

Playing Dead is Fun!

I wrapped Rebecca in a hug and planted a sweet kiss on her cheek. "I'm sorry, I couldn't let anything happen to you. You mean so much to me. Let me use my magic to restore your heart and soul," she said. Taking her magic mirror, she opened it wider and shone my undead reflection in my face. I tried to look away from the melting light, but I felt hypnotized. My unwanted spirit left my body and into the small mirror. I became mortal, myself again. I jumped with joy.

But our celebration got interrupted when the other angry mod of Moon Goonies *swiped* the Miracle Mirror out of Rebecca's reach. It fell into the mess next to the refreshment. Where the deejay tried to get it. But a dead zombie foot stepped on his hand. He screamed and tried to free his hand, when the young male undead boy used his other free foot and *smashed* Rebecca's mirror he saw under the rumble.

Crying out in shock, we watched as all the souls my girlfriend saved got freed of her Miracle Mirror and went back to where they belong too. We watched as Hunter, Tonya, and Christina got brought back to life. They leaped to their feet and couldn't feel happier.

"So, who's for lunch?" Hunter growled. Grabbing hold of his stomach, trying to control his unbearable hunger. Their Behavior Bracelets continued flashing red. And they all started laughing. Nervous, laughter. Even though I knew I would never get used to being an unappreciative undead, soulless thing, to walk the earth for eternity.

ABOUT THE AUTHOR

Jeremy Robertson enjoys reading or writing, hanging out with family and friends, and keeping an entertaining agenda. Jeremy grew up in a small Texas town. He loves stories, they excite him! They transport him to other worlds!

Vist Mr. Robertson at:

https://www.jeremysscarylibrary.com !

THE END?

Made in the USA
Columbia, SC
06 March 2021